I'm a Girl!

Lila Jukes
illustrated by Susan Keeter

COOL KIDS
P R E S S
Boca Raton, Florida

Text copyright ©1995 by Lila Jukes
Illustrations copyright ©1995 by Susan Keeter

ISBN: 1-56790-519-6

First Printing

COOL KIDS PRESS

1098 N.W. Boca Raton Boulevard, Suite 1
Boca Raton, FL 33432

Jukes, Lila, 1962
    I'm a girl! / Lila Jukes ; illustrated by Susan Keeter.
      p. cm.
    Summary: Girls make statements affirming their value, talent, strength and courage.
    ISBN 1-56790-519-6. -- ISBN 1-56790-518-8 (pbk.)
    [1. Self acceptance--Fiction. 2. Self-perception--Fiction.]
  I. Keeter, Susan, ill. II. Title.
PZ7.J9293Ij   1995
[E]--dc20   95-18189
                                 CIP
                                 AC

For my daughter,
and for all the
other spectacular women
of tomorrow.

– L.J.

For Mary Faulk Markiewicz,
who taught me a love of old houses,
good books, and strong characters.

– S.K.

I'm a strong girl,

strong enough to run in the waves,

strong enough to hit
the ball over the fence,

strong enough to dance and leap
and feel like I'm flying.

I'm a brave and courageous girl,

courageous enough to sing loud and clear,

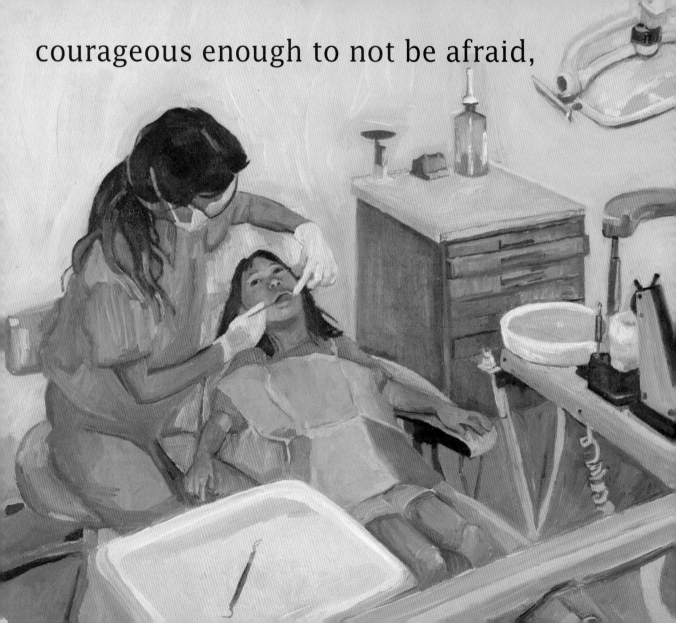

courageous enough to not be afraid,

courageous enough to make a new friend.

I'm a powerful girl,

powerful enough
to make my
baby brother
smile when no one
else can,

powerful enough to say no to things
that could hurt me,

powerful enough to create
something wonderful.

I'm a smart girl,

smart enough to solve all the problems
on the board,

smart enough to make everybody laugh
when I say something funny,

smart enough to remember when it's my mom's birthday.

I'm an independent girl,

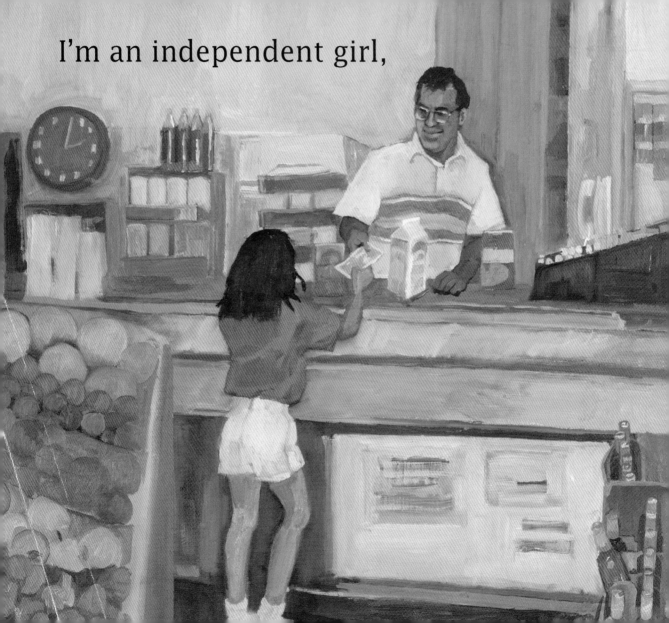

independent enough to like doing new
things all by myself,

independent enough to take care of
someone else,

independent enough to cheer myself up when I'm feeling blue.

valuable enough to be loved and cherished,

valuable enough to eat good foods
that will make me strong,

valuable enough to tell the truth
about my feelings.

And because I'm strong and courageous,

because I'm smart and powerful,

because I'm independent and valuable...

I'm beautiful.

E
Jukes   Jukes, Lila

I'm a girl!

DUE DATE	BRODART	04/96	13.95

5/2/96